AN ABC

OF WHAT ART CAN BE

Meher McArthur

Pictures by Esther Pearl Watson

The J. Paul Getty Museum, Los Angeles

is for ARTIST,
creator of art,

making all sorts of things
with the hands and the heart.

B is for BRUSH,
used to paint or to write

On a wall or a page
or a canvas of white.

C's for COMPUTER.
If there's one in your house,
it can help you make art—
with the click of a mouse!

meow

Click

D

Make DRAWINGS
with pencils or crayons
or chalk—
on paper...on cardboard...
or on the sidewalk.*

Cat

Hamster

H

*Ask First

E's for EXPRESSION,
your personal style.
You might find it soon,
or it might take a while.

A FRAME can be
a work of art, too:

whether bought at a store—
or made by YOU.

G is for GOLD, the color of kings. It's used to make some of our most precious things.

make a wish!

H

is for HIEROGLYPHS.
For "trees," "fish," or "birds,"
Egyptians wrote symbols
the way we write words.

INSPIRATION!

An idea so clever,
   it helps you come up with
your best artwork ever.

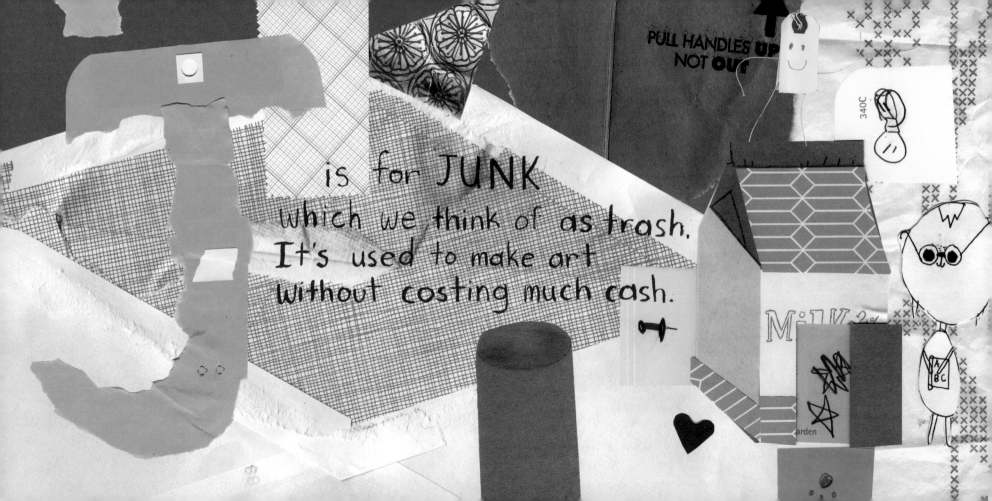

is for JUNK
which we think of as trash.
It's used to make art
without costing much cash.

is for KILN,
an oven that's hot.
You can bake clay inside it
and make a nice pot.

is for LANDSCAPE,
a beautiful scene,
of rivers and mountains
and pastures of green.

M's for MUSEUM,
where art is displayed—
like mobiles... or masks...
things artists have made.

is for NEEDLE—
for sewing with thread.
Make a hat, a wall hanging...
a quilt for your bed.

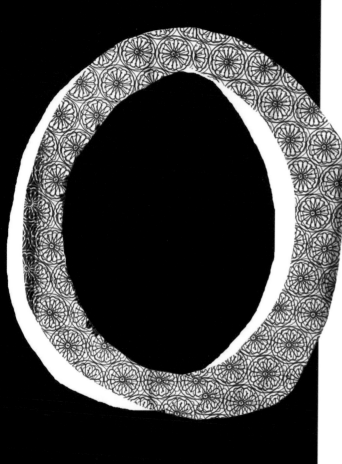

's ORIGAMI,
which comes from Japan.
Fold paper to make
your own bird, boat, or fan.

is for PRINTS
that you may want to make—
of your friends...
or your scooter...
or your **dog**'s birthday cake...

Q is for QUESTION:
"What can it be?"
To you, it's a person;
to me, it's a tree!

's for ROUGH DRAFT,
a quick first design.
Erase it! Redo it! —
until it's just fine.

is for SCULPTURE,
a work in 3-D.
Make it small as a button
or big as a tree.

T is for TONE,
meaning darker or lighter:
A color can change
as it slowly gets brighter.

is **UNIQUE** —
it's one-of-kind.
An artwork that's like it
you never will **find**.

is for **VANISHING POINT:**
it's the dot
where lines seem to meet,
far away, at one spot.

is for WEAVING.
With a light touch
you can make your own
baskets...and bookmarks...
and such.

X

X-HIBITION
(really spelled with an E).
It's where art is shown
for people to see.

EXHIBITION
TODAY

Y is for YARN
much loved by kittens,
and knitters of scarves,
socks, blankets, and
mittens.

Z is for ZILLIONS
of ways to make art.
Pick a pencil, a color, a fabric—
and **START**!!!!

Crayo

Crayon

FUN STUFF

NOTE 1: You may need to ask a grownup for a little help with some of these.

NOTE 2: If you have to use glue, be sure to use NONTOXIC glue. Just to be safe.

1.
Make your own X-hibition—that is, Exhibition! Ask your friends and classmates to create artworks. Then make frames or stands for each and ask your teacher if you can show them in your classroom. Where else could you have your exhibition?

2.
How many hands (and how many paws!) did you find in the pictures in this book? Hands are what we use most often to create art. Could we use other parts of our bodies to make art?

3.
There's a basic pattern to weaving anything—a shirt, a rug, a basket. And the pattern is: over 1, under 1; over 1, under 1. That's what happens as one thread weaves around another. (You can see it in this illustration.) Look around your house to find five things that are woven with the "over 1, under 1" pattern. How would you weave something yourself? What would you need?

4.

All through history, people have made masks that look like animals or scary monsters. Find a paper plate, some paint, feathers, string, or beads, and then use tape or glue to make the scariest face you can imagine. Or the funniest!

6.

Paint brushes are sometimes made from animal hair, but you can also make them from other things: feathers, leaves, grass, and even small twigs. Tape some to a small stick or pencil and see what kind of pictures you can paint!

5.

People all over the world make impressions of things like leaves, stones, and sticks. You can, too. First flatten out some clay. (Be sure the clay is the kind that dries fast and can be painted.) Then find some interesting leaves—grape, sycamore, maple—and press them onto the surface of the clay to create leaf prints. When the clay is dry, you can paint the leaves any colors you like—red, yellow, purple, blue!

7.

In China and Japan, paper-tearing has been an art form for hundreds of years. Find as many different kinds of paper as you can—newspaper, old holiday cards, Japanese washi paper, gift wrap, brown paper lunch bags—and tear out different shapes, patterns, and pictures. (No scissors! The whole point is to tear, not cut.) Use glue or tape to stick them onto a large piece of white paper to create your own work of art—or a card for someone's birthday.

8.

Make your own frame for your pictures or photographs. Paint four popsicle sticks your favorite color and then glue them together to form a square or rectangle. (Or use three to make a triangle.) Decorate the frame with stickers, glitter, and beads. Put a picture or photo on a card and then put your frame around it. See how different it looks now!

9.

Portraits are usually pictures of people. Draw a portrait of someone you know—a family member, a friend, even a pet. Then ask them to draw one of YOU. (This may be hard for your dog to do.)

10.
What kind of landscape do you live in? A farm? A forest? A city? Or somewhere else? What colors and shapes would you use to paint a picture of it?

12.
Many artists make art out of junk. Create your own work of art out of boxes, packages, string, bottle tops, wrappers, tape, envelopes, an empty milk carton—anything at all. (Make sure it's clean.) It's a great way to recycle!

11.
Everyone has their own personal style. What's yours? How do you decorate your room? How do you dress? Do you like bright colors, dark colors, a combination of the two? With colored pencils, crayons, or paint on paper, come up with a room, or a dress, or a shirt, or even a pillowcase, that shows your style!

13.
The ancient Egyptians wrote and drew on pieces of papyrus (made from the papyrus plant)—which is where we get the word *paper*.

They wrote with pictures called *hieroglyphs*. Try making up your own. How would you write "I ride a bicycle to school" in hieroglyphs? Can you create a secret code with your friends using hieroglyphs?

14.
Make your t-shirt into art. Find one of your old t-shirts and make it new again by printing, drawing, or using new ideas you have found in this book. Make it all about you!

Click

15.
If you're near a computer, visit the Getty's website to find more ideas for art to make at home....just click on your mouse!

http://getty.edu/ gettygames/downloads

Have fun!